Martinis & Mysteries

The Boozy Book Club Series

By

Rose Bak

Also by Rose Bak

Bite-Sized Shifters
Long Distance Wolf
Wolf Doctor
Kat's Dog
Designer Wolf
Wolf Sheriff
Cocktail Wolf
Second Chance Wolf

Boozy Book Club
Beach Reads
Bubbly & Billionaires: A Midlife Instalove Romantic Comedy
Martinis & Mysteries

Diamond Bay
Brand New Penny
Fresh as a Daisy
Right as Rain

Good With Numbers
Love Unmasked
The Thanksgiving Scrooge
Maid for Christmas
Countdown to Love
Valentine's Lottery

Holidays With the Shifters
Santa's Claws
Bear Humbug
Jingle Bear
Joy to the Wolf
Lion's Heart
Silver Paws

Loving the Holidays
Dating Santa
New Year's Steve
Independence Dave

Magical Midlife Romance
Love Potion

Oliver Boys Band

Until You Came Along
Rock Star Teacher
Rock Star Writer
Rock Star Neighbor

Reunited
Together Again
Finding My Baby

Self-Help for the Real World
It's All About Relationships

Standalone
What to Do If You Find a Cougar in Your Living Room
Beach Wedding
Good with Numbers
Christmas Love Stories: A Holiday Romance Anthology
Diamond Bay
Christmas with the Shifters

Watch for more at https://rosebakenterprises.com/.

Table of Contents

About This Book

Cops in romance books are always so sweet and protective. Unfortunately, Evie's life is no romance book.

Bookstore owner Evie Fontenot has a mystery to solve. Someone is messing with her bookstore, and there's no way someone is going to get away with ruining the successful business she created. Her friends insist she report the issues to the police, but based on her history with the law, she knows they'll be no help. When she meets the bossy and rigid police chief, she knows she's right.

Jake Wilson isn't sure what's going on at Boozy Books, but there's one thing he does know: Evie is the woman he's been looking for his whole life. He doesn't appreciate Evie's "girl detective" act or her prickly independence, but he does appreciate her business savvy and generous curves.

At their age, there's no reason to play games. But Evie has no interest in forever, and he's not interested in settling for anything less.

"Martinis & Mysteries" is book two in the "Boozy Book Club" series. Each story in the series is a steamy standalone featuring a couple in their fifties, a nosy group of book club friends, matchmaking family members, and a sweet happily ever after that proves anyone can find love later in life.

This book includes a special excerpt from "Until You Came Along", book one of the Oliver Boys Rockstar series, available now from all major online retailers.

Be sure to join Rose's mailing list and get a free book. Click here[1] to be the first to hear about all the latest releases and special sales.

---

1.   https://storyoriginapp.com/giveaways/62ee758e-068f-11eb-904e-c373f6014fe1

Dedication

To Scooby and the gang. You meddling kids brought us a lot of joy in our youth. And to my favorite girl detective, Nancy Drew. You were ahead of your time.

Prologue—Evie

One month ago...

I looked around at the small crowd of women scattered around the café area of my bookstore and felt a surge of pride. I'd literally built this place up from nothing.

Five years ago, my husband had left me for another woman. I hadn't seen it coming. Hadn't had a clue that he'd been cheating on me for a long time. When he came home one day and announced he wanted out of our twenty year marriage like it'd mean nothing, my legs had buckled from the shock. I'd sat on the kitchen floor, staring up at my husband blankly as he calmly destroyed my life, our life, the life we'd built together, with a careless indifference that still made my chest hurt when I thought about it.

Paul had given me the house in the settlement, moving in with his girlfriend a few towns over but that was all I walked away with. My friends told me I should have sued him for alimony – after all, it was at his insistence that I'd been a stay at home mom to our daughter. Even after Nicole had grown up and gone away from college, I'd dedicated myself to being a good wife. I'd focused my time on being a volunteer so I could be available for my husband and his needs.

I was such a sucker.

Destitute and desperate, I'd floundered for a bit, taking any random temp job I could get to bring in some money. I felt directionless until I heard that Mrs. and Mrs. Peterson were selling their bookstore on Main Street and moving to Florida to retire. I'd spent many happy hours hanging around the shop, and I'd even worked there for a while in high school and college. When Mrs. Peterson told me the news, I'd begged them to hold off on announcing the sale and to give me first shot at buying it.

I couldn't qualify for a business loan. According to the bank, being a wife, mother, and professional volunteer did nothing to prepare me to run a business, despite my business degree. On a whim I set up one of those crowdsourcing sites to raise the capital I needed. It'd been a Hail Mary, but it had paid off. The people of this town had rallied around me, donating their money as well as sharing links to the fundraiser all over social media. I couldn't believe that total strangers in other states would donate to help me, and I was grateful for the support. When it was done, I had myself a bookstore.

I'd re-tooled the shop, changing the name to Boozy Books, opening up the space and expanding our selection of books. I'd also converted an unused loft space to a café that served coffee and pastries in the morning, and wine, beer, and sandwiches in the later hours. My best friends Emma and Dawn had helped me freshen the place up, opening up walls, painting, and doing anything we didn't need a licensed professional to do. I'd worked through a lot of my anger about the divorce while taking a sledgehammer to walls in the store.

The store took off, attracting both locals and the tourists who flocked to our beachfront town. I'd soon added an online store that was even more popular than the physical site.

I'd started the Boozy Book Club about a year after I took over the bookstore. The premise was simple: each month we would combine some kind of an alcoholic beverage with a book. Last month our theme had been "Bubbly & Billionaires" and we'd paired champagne cocktails with a billionaire romance that was so hot I swear my e-reader was smoking at times.

I charged book club members a small fee to cover the cost of the refreshments, and even though they could get the book of the month at the library, everyone bought the books at my store. It had turned into a profitable little enterprise, and our numbers were growing by the month as word of mouth spread.

The conversation about our billionaire book was wrapping up and it was time to announce the selections for the next month. We all took turns coming up with a book and a matching beverage, but this month it was my turn to make the selection. I stood up and whistled to capture everyone's attention.

"Thank you for coming tonight," I announced. "I hope you all enjoyed this month's theme of Bubbly and Billionaires."

I winked at my friend Emma who'd recently fell head over heels for her own billionaire. They'd gotten together pretty fast, but she seemed happy, so I was thrilled for her.

"Our theme for next month is Martinis and Mysteries, and we're going to be reading 'The Mystery of Cedar Cove'. It's a cozy mystery featuring a trio of amateur sleuths, and I think you'll all enjoy it. We have copies available for purchase at the check-out area. Enjoy your reading ladies, and as always, thanks for supporting the Boozy Book Club."

As the book club members lined up at the register to purchase the next book, Emma and Dawn helped me clean up the café. As we finished off the rest of the champagne cocktail that we'd served the book club, Emma gave me and Dawn a sly smile.

"Now that I found someone, maybe it's time for the two of you to get out there too."

Dawn and I groaned. I'd dated a ton after my divorce, but the last year or so I'd stopped, tired of the games. I was fifty-one years old and the guys I met were either looking for thirty year olds or a nursemaid. I was neither of those things. Since I'd stepped off the dating merry-go-round, it was just me and my trusty vibrator.

"Just because you found a great guy doesn't mean Dawn and I have to torture ourselves," I reminded her. "You know dating sucks at our age."

"Besides, we're both busy business owners," Dawn added. She ran a successful seafood restaurant down by the Promenade and I had the bookstore.

Emma gave us the "don't argue with me" stare that she'd perfected as a nurse.

"All I'm saying is that it's never too late to find love."

"It is for me," I responded.

Emma shook her head. "I really hope you're wrong Evie. I didn't realize what was missing in my life until I found Wyatt. I just hate for you to be alone for the rest of your life."

I placed one hand on her shoulder and one on Dawn's. "I'm not alone. I've got you two."

Evie

"What the hell?"

I walked in the door and looked around my store in confusion. Someone had knocked over a bookshelf, sending books to the floor in a messy heap. Two other shelves were still upright, but most of their contents were on the floor. Had I been robbed?

I moved behind the check-out area. The two cash registers and computers were still in place, although they didn't have any money in them anyway. I wasn't an idiot. I kept all the money in a safe in the back office.

The back office...I headed there and was relieved to see it looked untouched. A glance at the storeroom across the hall showed it was also fine. I heard water running and headed into the customer restroom. The faucet was running full blast, although thankfully the water was all going down the drain and not on my tile. I looked up and saw that someone had wrote "get out!" in what looked like lipstick on the mirror.

I texted Emma and Dawn to share the news. They were my ride-or-die friends, and we shared everything.

Evie: *OMFG someone was in the shop last night!*

Dawn: *Were you robbed?*

Evie: *Not that I can tell. They knocked a bunch of shit off the shelves and left the water running in the bathroom. Oh, and there's this.*

I attached a picture of the bathroom mirror and the lipstick message.

Emma: *Call the cops!*

Evie: *Why? You know they don't do shit.*

Emma: *Call them, or I will. What if they come back and hurt you?*

Evie: *You know I hate cops.*

My father had been a cop. He'd also been an abusive male-chauvinist asshole who I'd cut ties with as soon as I was old enough to be out on my own. If my asshole father wasn't enough to make me hate cops, the way that the local cops in the town I grew up in did nothing when my mother called them after one beating too many had cemented my hatred of the boys in blue. A couple of years after I left home my mother had finally left him, taking my sister Teresa with her.

Dawn: *Evie, it's your business. Besides, you'll need documentation of a police report if you have to file an insurance claim. Do it, and text us later and let us know how you are.*

Evie: *Fine. I'll talk to you later.*

I looked around once more before calling the non-emergency police line.

"Chief Wilson is in the area Ms. Fontenot, I'll send him over now."

"Thank you."

Five minutes later a burly man in a blue police uniform strode into my bookstore like he owned the place. I looked up at him and caught my breath. Good Lord, he was a fine looking man.

He looked like he was in his early fifties, same as me. He was tall, at least several inches taller than my own five foot eight height, with broad shoulders, biceps that strained against the thin blue fabric of his police uniform, and legs like tree trunks. He had hair that was somewhere between brown and blond, cut short and threaded through with silver, a short salt and pepper beard covering his sharp jaw, sensuous lips, and those damn reflective sunglasses cops loved to wear. Then he removed the glasses, sticking them into the collar of his uniform shirt, and revealed curious brown eyes flanked with long brown eyelashes.

"Miss Phone-ten-not?" He asked, mangling my name as he read it off his cell phone.

"It's pronounced 'fonn-ta-noh.'"

He looked between me and his phone, frowning slightly like he thought I was messing with him. He really had the cop look down: a mixture of stern and arrogant.

"I'm Chief Jake Wilson," he said. "I don't believe we've met."

He reached forward to shake my hand. It was the weirdest thing, but it felt like everything inside me stilled the minute our hands touched.

Except for the skin on my hands, which felt warm and tingly everywhere it touched his. He looked up and met my eyes, looking almost as confused as I felt.

After just a touch too long, we both pulled away.

He cleared his throat. "I understand you've had a break-in?"

I showed him around, pointing out the things that were messed up. He checked the locks on both doors, confirming what I already knew: no one had tampered with them. As we moved through the store, he made notes in a little notepad that he pulled out of his pocket.

"Do you think you left a door unlocked?" he said.

"No, I didn't."

"Are you sure?" His tone was patronizing, and it raised my ire.

"Both doors were locked when I got here," I said firmly, giving him a hard look.

"And they didn't take the computers or the cash registers? That's weird."

"I don't keep cash in them anyway, but I agree that it's strange. But there's also this."

I led him into the restroom. "The water was running, but I turned that off. And this message was on the mirror."

He frowned. "That looks personal. Do you know anyone who would want to harm your business?"

"No," I said. "I don't have enemies."

We wandered back to the front of the store.

"Well, there's not a lot to go on here," he said. "But I'll file a report."

He turned as if to leave, and I looked at him incredulously.

"Not a lot to go on? Can't you dust for fingerprints? Take pictures? Do anything?"

"I said I'd file a report," he said mildly. "There's no sign of a break-in. This looks like some kind of a prank to me."

I threw up my hands. "I knew it was a waste of time to call you. I should know better than expect cops to actually do their damn jobs."

I stalked away and started pushing on the shelf that had been knocked over, trying to get it upright again. It didn't budge until Chief Wilson came over to help.

"I got it," I snapped, but he ignored me. Which was probably good, because honestly, it was too heavy for me to move by myself.

I glanced out of the corner of my eye, noting how his biceps bulged with the effort. It was too bad he was a jerk and a cop because Chief Wilson was one fine specimen. Shaking my head, I started reshelving the books, ignoring him.

He stood there awkwardly before finally saying, "Give us a call if anything else happens."

I turned to him and gave him my best glare. "If anything else happens, I'll investigate it my own damn self instead of wasting time with you."

I wondered if it was possible to buy fingerprinting kits online. I'd check into that, as well as security cameras. It wasn't something I expected to need in a town where half the people didn't even lock their doors at night.

"Now we don't need you going all Nancy Drew on us," he said sternly. "You leave the police work to the experts."

"Yeah, I'm super impressed by you experts," I practically spat at him. "Now get the hell out of my store!"

With one last stern glare, he turned on his heel and headed for the door.

Jake

They say that there comes a time in every man's life when something happens that will change their life forever. After fifty-two years, it finally had happened to me. I was in love. I was a goner the minute I saw her, even if she obviously wasn't that impressed with me. Yet.

"Now get the hell out of my store!"

Evie's face was red with anger, but she was still the most beautiful woman I'd ever seen. And I'd seen plenty of women in my life. She was about a head shorter than my six foot one, with a curvy body that I couldn't wait to get my hands on.

Evie was dressed in tight black leggings that showed off her muscled legs and thick thighs. She wore a loose floral-patterned shirt that was left open, showing the tight pink tank top beneath. Full breasts strained the fabric, and I could see the indent of her trim waist. She wore at least a half a dozen bracelets on each wrist, a combination of beads and bangles.

But it was her face that convinced me that love at first sight really existed. Her face was heart-shaped, with a pointy little chin just below full red lips. Evie had defined cheek bones and large brown eyes, clear of make-up, with eyebrows that arched just enough to look like she was asking a question every time she looked at me. Her hair was a chestnut brown, almost black, cut in a blunt bob, with several bright pink streaks. She was quirky, breathtaking, and soon -—she would be mine. She just didn't know it yet.

If there was one thing I'd learned during my twenty years in the military, it was the value of a strategic retreat. I headed towards the door, sliding a business card onto the counter near the cash register.

"Give me a call if anything else weird happens," I repeated firmly.

"Yeah, right," she mumbled.

I stopped by the door and turned to face her. "Call me." I ordered in my best authoritative cop voice.

She rolled her eyes and waved her hand towards the door. "Goodbye now."

I couldn't help but smile as I walked down the street and headed back towards the police station that sat right at the edge of the main street downtown. It was a great little town, and I liked it a lot. It reminded me of the town where I'd grown up.

After doing my twenty in the military, part of that as military police, I'd retired and got a job in law enforcement in Atlanta. I stayed there for a few years until I had enough time under my belt to get the job I'd always dreamed of: small town police chief.

I'd moved here about a year ago to take the police chief role, but somehow I'd never seen Evie Fontenot before. I wasn't much of a reader, to be honest, so I'd never had a reason to stop by her bookstore. That was going to change real quick. My Evie was quite the spitfire. I couldn't wait to get to know her better.

I entered the station and smiled at Marci, our dispatcher.

"Did you check out the break-in at the bookstore, Chief?" she asked.

"Yeah. Looks like a prank or something."

Marci frowned. "I hope so. Poor Evie has been through enough, she doesn't need anyone messing with her livelihood."

Recognizing an opportunity to get information about my future wife from the gossipy dispatcher, I leaned on the corner of her desk. "What do you mean?"

Marci gave me a considering look, no doubt wondering why I'd shut down all of her other attempts at gossip until today.

"She had a rough childhood, from what I hear. She moved here with her husband after they got married. He was one of those who insisted that his wife needed to stay home with their kid, then he cheated on her for years before he dumped her for some chippy half his age. Left her with nothing but their house. No income, no savings, nothing."

"Wow."

"She bounced around doing odd jobs for a while, then the Petersons announced they were retiring and moving to Florida. Evie used to work for them when she was a kid, and she spent a lot of time at that store over the years, so she asked them to sell it to her. Our Evie's a smart one. When she couldn't get a business loan, she did a big fundraising thing online, and got enough money to buy the store and do the remodeling to add the café on top. I think everyone in town contributed. She also set up an online store, and I hear the business makes much more profit than it did when the Petersons ran it."

"How do you know that?"

"My nephew is her accountant."

I shook my head, wondering at the gossip network in small towns.

"So, um, she's single then?"

The gleam in Marci's eyes told me that this question would be all over town in half an hour. Maybe less. She leaned forward.

"She's done a lot of dating, but never anyone serious, not since her divorce."

Before she could ask me any questions, I thanked her and pushed off her desk, heading towards my office to do some paperwork. It was shocking how much paperwork was involved in being chief. And if I periodically stopped to daydream about Evie, well, that was my secret.

I spent a restless night trying to figure out how to get close to Evie. I knew instinctively that she wouldn't make it easy for me. But I'd seen her eyeing my biceps and staring at me when she thought I wasn't looking, and that gave me hope.

The next morning, I couldn't keep myself from stopping by the bookstore. I told myself that it was just to make sure she didn't have any more trouble, but I was lying. The truth was, I was dying to see her. I hadn't stopped thinking about her since I saw her the day before.

When I walked into the store, the first thing I saw was Evie's heart-shaped ass sticking up in the air. My dick twitched as I saw her on hands and knees, scrubbing at the floor. I had a sudden flash of me taking

Evie from behind and had to take a deep breath to calm down before I was rocking a hard-on.

I cleared my throat and she looked at me over her shoulder. Her face hardened as soon as she saw it was me. I glanced past her to see she was cleaning red paint off the floor.

"What happened?" I asked.

She pushed up to sit on her heels. Today she was wearing faded jeans with a dark red short-sleeved knit top. Bracelets jangled on both wrists.

"Someone broke in again and spraypainted 'get out' on my damn tile," she snapped. "It's a pain in the ass to clean off."

"Why didn't you call it in to the station?" I asked.

"Because you did nothing yesterday, so why would I waste my time?"

I strode over to get a closer look. I could still see the faint outline of the words 'get out' on the tile despite what looked like vigorous scrubbing.

"Tell me everything."

She sighed and pushed to standing, lifting her chin to meet my eyes. We were only like a foot apart, and for a second, I completely forgot what we were talking about. Her eyes were fascinating, dark brown but they seemed to have gold flecks that I hadn't noticed yesterday. My heart sped up.

"I tripled checked the locks before I left last night," she told me, her voice dripping with annoyance. "Both doors were still locked when I came in today, but there was this little love note."

She pointed to the paint on the ground.

"Anything else messed with?"

"No."

I pulled out my little notebook and took notes. "What time did you leave last night."

"Nine o'clock."

I looked at my watch, noting that it was just before ten a.m.

"Who else has keys?"

"Just me."

"Your staff?"

She shook her head. "I have a few part-timers, but I'm always here to open and close."

"When do you take a day off?" I asked curiously. I hoped she wasn't working too hard.

"Not your business, Chief." She sneered the last word, like it was a curse.

"It's Jake."

"Huh?"

"My first name is Jake. I know you said you think you don't have any enemies, but what about any ex-boyfriends?"

"Maybe I date women," she sassed. "Did you think about that?"

Actually, I hadn't. I assumed she was straight based on what Marci had told me yesterday.

"Do you have any ex-boyfriends or ex-girlfriends who might be angry with you?" I amended.

"Nope, I don't date anyone long enough to get serious."

I was dying to ask more about that but forced myself to focus on my job instead.

"I'm going to ask the night shift to drive by a few times tonight and check on things," I told her.

"Yeah. Okay." Her voice clearly indicated that she wasn't impressed with my offer.

I closed the distance between us and placed my hand on her arm. My palm tingled from the contact. Evie's eyes widened and she looked confused, letting me know that she felt this attraction simmering between us as much as I did.

"Call me if anything else happens," I ordered.

"Why? So you can write about it in your little notebook again?"

My girl had a mouth on her and damned if I didn't like it.

"I mean it."

She stepped back, her expression rebellious and stubborn.

"I've got to finish cleaning this up and I haven't even had any coffee yet. You can show yourself out."

And with that, she flounced towards the back of the store, leaving me staring at her shapely ass.

The next morning, I showed up just before ten, carrying two coffees. Amy at the Daily Grind had kindly shared what Evie's favorite coffee was, even though I knew it would be all over town that I asked. But then again, maybe a little matchmaking would help me get my girl. She clearly didn't like me. I was determined to change that and wasn't above buttering her up with coffee to make some headway.

I headed into the store and found Evie sweeping up glass near a display case.

"What happened now?"

She jumped, so intent on her task she hadn't heard me come up behind her. Turning, she gave me that annoyed look that made my dick take notice.

"What are you doing here?"

"Just checking to see if there were any more problems. Patrol didn't notice anything weird last night."

She waved at the broken glass from the display case that held rare books. "Well, your patrol clearly did a great job since the bandit struck again."

"Damn it."

I put the coffees on a nearby table and examined the cabinet carefully. The glass was broken, and someone had left a piece of paper on the shelf with the same message as the other ones: 'get out'.

"Still think this is still a prank?" she snapped.

"I guess not." I sighed. I didn't like crime happening in my town. "I'll add this to the report."

She just rolled her eyes at me. I straightened and handed her one of the cups.

"What's this?" she asked suspiciously.

"Nonfat caramel macchiato. Amy said it was your favorite."

She took the cup, sniffing it before taking a careful sip. Her eyes closed and a look of pleasure crossed her face as she tasted the coffee. I was mesmerized by that look. I decided right then and there to make it my mission in life to put that look on her face every day for the rest of my life.

Evie

Damn it. It was hard to be mad at a guy who brought you coffee. At least until he opened his big fat mouth and said something annoying.

"You need to change the locks right away," he ordered in that bossy tone that made me want to smack him. And for the record, I was not a violent person.

I rolled my eyes. "You need to mind your own business."

"Crime in this town is my business."

Ignoring him, I set my coffee down and finished sweeping the broken glass into a paper bag, throwing the little love note from the vandal on top of the shards. I grabbed the bag, broom, and dustpan and stalked to the back room where I kept the trash. Dumping it into the can, I turned around and jumped. Chief Wilson was right behind me. That was the third time in two days that he'd snuck up on me.

"For such a big guy, you're awfully light on your feet," I grumbled. "Also, this area is for employees only."

"Ms. Fontenot. Evie. Please, promise me you'll change the locks," he said, his voice softer than I'd heard it. "It's clear that someone got a key somehow and is using it to cause trouble."

I sighed deeply.

"Not that it's any of your business, but I have the locksmith coming today."

He nodded. "Good. That should take care of it."

I expected him to leave, but he stood there watching me instead. Something about the way he was looking at me was making me nervous.

"What?" I asked belligerently.

He stepped closer, until only a few inches separated us. It forced me to lift my head to meet his gaze. His eyes looked almost...tender.

"Have dinner with me."

I reared back in shock. "What?"

"I'm asking you out."

"That sounded like ordering, not asking."

His lips twitched like he wanted to smile but didn't know how. Gruff was clearly his default setting.

"Evie, would you please have dinner with me?" he asked again.

I shook my head and stepped around him, ignoring the part of me that was thrilled by his invitation.

"No. Thanks for asking but I'm not interested."

My body had a different opinion, but I was using my head for once. Yay me. I'd dated a lot since my divorce, and had a lot of fun, but I knew instinctively that there was no way I could have my usual "one and done" with this man.

There was something about him that was way too appealing, despite his annoying personality. Jake had been occupying my thoughts ever since the first day I laid eyes on him, and I didn't like that. Not at all. The last thing I wanted was to let some guy have space in my head. The last time I'd done that I'd found myself divorced, unemployed, and broke.

I stalked out of the storeroom and Jake followed me back into the store, a little closer than I was comfortable with. I swear he was close enough that I could feel the heat of his body across my back. I stopped and turned on my heel to face him.

"Hey Chief, ever hear of personal space?" I waved my hands between us. "I like a three foot bubble at all times."

He stepped back but continued to stare at me in a way that a bit unnerving. It felt like he could look right into my head, which was a ridiculous thought.

"You don't feel this attraction between us?" He waved at the space between us, as if to highlight the energy shimmering between us. "I can't be the only one feeling this."

"I don't date cops," I answered, sidestepping the question.

One eyebrow raised. "Now this is a story I'd love to hear."

"Too bad. I need to get ready to open the store now, so if you don't mind...well, you know where the door is."

"Call me if anything else happens. You don't have to handle this all by yourself."

When I didn't respond, he stalked back towards me, his face set in that stern look that every cop perfected by the time they left the academy.

"Evie."

"Chief." I mimicked.

"I'll check on you later," he growled. He turned to leave, and I was absolutely not watching the fabric stretch across the muscles of his ass. Not at all.

I was cranky as hell when I got up the next morning. I'd gotten totally immersed in this month's book club book, 'The Mystery of Cedar Cove'.

The book really pulled you in. I read so much that I could usually figure out who the criminal was early on in any book, but not this one. It had a lot of twists and turns as well as some hot as hell sex scenes between the main female sleuth and the hot cop who wanted her off the case. By the time I finally went to bed I was just as confused about the crook as I had been when I started reading.

It had to be because of the book that I'd had a vivid sex dream about Chief Jake Wilson. There was no other reason.

I used my new key to unlock the door, holding my breath as I looked around the store, checking for anything out of place. I breathed a sigh of relief when I saw everything was as it should be.

A few minutes before ten my new friend Chief Wilson wandered in, once again holding two cups of coffee. Today he was dressed in civilian clothes. Faded jeans hugged his thighs lovingly, and a Carolina Panthers shirt stretched across his impressive chest and arms.

"Macchiato?" he asked, handing me the cup.

"Thank you," I said grudgingly.

"Any problems last night?" he asked, studying me with those perceptive brown eyes.

"Nope." I took a sip of the coffee and suppressed a groan. "Why are you dressed like a normal person?"

"I'm off weekends."

I nodded.

"What time do you close tonight?"

"Five o'clock." We closed earlier on weekends.

"Can I buy you dinner?" he asked. "I'd like to get to know you better."

I shook my head. My body was screaming "Go out with him. Climb him like a tree!" but my head was telling me to stay as far away from him as I could. If there was one thing I'd learned over the last few years, it was that I had to listen to my head.

"Look, I'm sure you're a nice guy..." This was a lie, I assumed all cops were assholes. "But I'm just not..."

My words fell off as he stepped closer, close enough that I could smell something citrusy, maybe his bodywash or his shampoo. Jake took the coffee cup out of my hand and set it on the counter, still giving me that unnerving stare. He reached up and pushed a strand of hair behind my ear. I shivered.

"I like your pink strips," he said, nodding at my hair.

I liked to change my hair color every so often. I'd recently swapped out my purple streaks for pink.

Jake cupped my cheek in one large palm, and it took everything in me not to lean into his touch. He lowered his head until our lips were an inch apart, and I felt myself swaying closer. Our lips touched, just for a few seconds, and it was enough to make my entire body come alive. I gasped, and jumped back, making some space between us.

"What were you saying about not being interested?" he asked cockily.

"Get out!" I pointed towards the door angrily. Jake gave me a smirk that made me tempted to punch him in the throat.

"I'll check on you tomorrow."

"Don't."

He walked backwards, watching me. "Now that we fixed your break-in problem, you need to know that I intend to date you, even if it takes some time to wear you down. I want you Evie, and I know I'm not the only one feeling this."

Before I could give him a piece of my mind, he was gone, leaving me gaping after him with an aching feeling in my core that I didn't want to think about too closely.

Jake

The next morning was Sunday, and as I headed downtown to check on Evie I had a little spring in my step. She might say she wasn't attracted to me, but the way she'd softened against my palm yesterday and swayed close enough for the quickest kiss in the history of kisses made me think she wasn't as immune to me as she thought she was.

Despite knowing at a cellular level that Evie was meant to be mine, I never would pursue her if I thought she truly wasn't interested. I wasn't a jerk. But her words and her actions didn't match. Yesterday when we'd been standing close, I could see her pulse pounding in the throat and her nipples had hardened against the thin fabric of her shirt. When she'd leaned forward to kiss me I knew the truth; she might be fighting it, but the attraction was there.

After grabbing our coffees, I walked over to her store. Evie was standing in front of the cash registers, looking pissed as hell. She was wearing a short knit black skirt over hot pink leggings, a darker pink shirt with a scoop neck hugging her breasts. She'd paired the outfit with Doc Martins and her signature combination of metal and beaded bracelets.

"What's wrong?" I asked.

Her eyes swung to me, then she pointed to the countertop. Someone had written 'get out' in large block letters, with what looked like black marker. They'd also taken a knife to the two chairs behind the counter, pulling the stuffing out of the backs and tossing it on the floor.

Whoever was messing with Evie was definitely determined, if not particularly original. I couldn't figure out why the vandal was going through this much trouble for relatively minor damage. It didn't make sense.

"I thought you changed the locks."

She huffed. "I did. I have no idea how they got in again."

I grabbed the radio that I always had with me and called into the station. "We have another break-in at the bookstore. Please send a uniform and a fingerprint kit."

Evie stomped away and returned a few minutes later with a plastic trash bag in her hand. Moving behind the desk, she started picking up stuffing off the floor and shoving it into the bag.

"You should leave that," I instructed.

She ignored me.

"Evie. You don't know if that's safe. At least wear gloves."

"I'm fine," she snapped.

I opened my mouth to argue, but the door opened. One of my officers, Dan Reyes, walked in and looked around cautiously, like he thought someone was going to jump him.

"Here, Reyes." I gestured to the top. "Can you wipe the counter down for fingerprints?"

"There's no fingerprints," Evie said. "I already checked."

"With what?"

"I bought a fingerprint kit on Amazon since the police weren't doing anything. The vandal must be wearing gloves."

"Well as impressive as that is, Nancy Drew, your kiddie fingerprint kit is not the same as ours."

She stopped picking up stuffing to glare at me. I glared right back. Our eyes were locked in a staring contest that neither of us wanted to lose.

"Uh, Chief?"

Reyes cleared his throat, making me look away, but not before I saw a look of triumph on Evie's face.

"There's nothing here."

"Score one for Nancy Drew," she crowed. "By the way, we have the whole series here if you want to learn more about doing investigations from everyone's favorite girl detective."

This time Reyes and I glared at her in tandem, but Evie just raised her eyebrows, clearly unafraid of us. Evie returned to picking up stuffing and after checking the front and back doors again and taking pictures, Reyes left to file his report.

Evie took the bag of stuffing to the back room, then returned with cleaning supplies. Without a word to me, she got started scrubbing the marker off the counter. I understood that Evie was frustrated with us, but we literally had nothing to go on here. I still hadn't ruled out this being some elaborate prank, although my instincts told me it was more.

"I left your coffee on that table," I finally said, pointing in the direction where I left her drink. "I can check on you tomorrow."

"I won't be here. We're closed on Mondays."

"What will you do on your day off?" I asked curiously.

"Try to solve a mystery, I guess." She frowned up at me, her forehead wrinkling.

"Call me if something else happens," I reminded her, even though she'd ignored me every other time. "I know you're frustrated that we haven't figured this out yet, but you need to let the professionals investigate this."

She shot me a salute and turned her attention back to the counter. With one last warning look, I marched out of the store and went home to enjoy the rest of my Sunday.

My phone rang around midnight that evening.

"Chief Wilson."

"Chief, it's Officer Johnston. I'm at the bookstore on patrol and I can see someone moving around in there. Dispatch said we were to call you right away if anything happened, day or night."

"Wait for me," I ordered. "I'll be there in five."

I threw on my shoes and grabbed my holster and service revolver, driving as fast as I could to Evie's bookstore. I parked on the corner and closed the remaining distance on foot. I found Johnston across the street, watching the windows closely.

"Do you have the master key?"

Every business in town had to have their locks keyed so our master would work in an emergency. We crossed the quiet street together, and I pressed my face against the glass, noticing a movement between the shelves. It was too dark to get much of an impression beyond that.

"I'll go in the back," I told Johnston. "You stay here and catch them if they leave through the front. Call for backup if things go south."

Not waiting for his response, I ran silently around the building, using the master key to open the back door. I crept past the storeroom and office and headed through the employee door that I knew led to the main store area. The door made a squeaking noise I hadn't expected.

I heard a female voice yell, "Freeze!" then I felt something hit my chest, hard enough to knock me off my feet. I fell to the ground, dropping my gun, just as someone turned on the overhead light.

It was Evie. She held a rifle in her hand, pointed in my direction. I looked down and saw a large red splotch of paint right over my heart. My girl was a good shot. Thank God she was using a paintball gun and not the real thing.

"Evie! What the HELL are you doing?" I bellowed as I rubbed my chest. Wet paint covered my hand, irritating me even more. I wiped it off on my tee shirt since it was ruined anyway.

"Oh my God, Jake! What are you doing here? You scared me half to death. I thought you were the vandal."

She dropped to her knees next to me, looking concerned, but held on tight to her paintball rifle.

"Did I hurt you?"

I pulled up my t-shirt and saw a nice bruise forming over my left pec.

"Nice shot," I grumbled. "You're damn lucky I didn't shoot you back."

Evie's mouth opened but no words came out. If I hadn't been so angry, I would have appreciated the way her eyes darkened as she checked out my chest and abs. I might have been in my fifties, but I worked hard to keep myself in shape.

I sat up and gripped her shoulders, not caring that I was smearing paint on her shirt. My mind was racing with what could have happened if it hadn't been me in the store if Evie's shot had missed. What if she'd gotten hurt by the intruder?

"What the hell were you doing in here with that? You could have been hurt or killed!"

She looked down at the paintball rifle in her hands, then back to me, going from worried to angry in five seconds. I wrestled it out of her hands and set it next to us on the ground next to the gun I'd dropped. Rookie mistake but I hadn't been expecting to be shot.

"I'm doing what the police won't do: figuring out who the hell is messing with my store!"

Still holding onto her shoulders, I dragged her closer and slammed my mouth down on hers. My kiss was hard and angry. I tightened my grip on her shoulders and bit her lower lip, demanding entrance. She made a squeaking noise, then opened for me. My tongue swept in, and she met me, our tongues dueling for control. My cock hardened painfully against my pants. I tilted my head to get a better angle as the kiss continued.

Our kiss was hot and almost violent. The way she was kissing me back told me two things: she was pissed as hell at me but liked the kiss as much as I did.

I heard footsteps and pulled away, panting. Evie sat back on her heels, chest rising as she gasped for breath. Her lips were as red and swollen as I imagined mine were. There was a paint handprint where I'd gripped her shoulder.

Johnston appeared, service weapon in hand but pointed at the ground. He stopped when he saw us sitting there in the back of the store, glaring at each other, and breathing heavily. He looked between us curiously.

"Um. Sorry Chief, I thought I heard something."

I gestured to my paint-splattered t-shirt.

Johnston's eyes widened as he took in the scene. "Someone shot you with a paintball rifle?"

I inclined my head towards Evie and Johnston puffed himself up to his full height.

"Do you want me to arrest her for assaulting an officer of the law?"

Evie

"Oh for fuck's sake! I didn't assault him on purpose! I thought he was a damn intruder! You can't just sneak into someone's business like that!"

I jumped to my feet and glared at the cop who looked young enough to be my kid.

Doogie Copper tightened his grip on his gun and looked to his boss. Jake pushed himself to standing with a grace that belied his size. His shirt fell back down, covering abs that were flatter than I would have expected. He was annoyingly attractive.

Oh my God, that kiss. I'm pretty sure we were like two minutes away from hate fucking if the kid cop hadn't interrupted us. My panties were drenched.

"We thought *you* were the intruder," the kid snapped back.

"How did you even get in here?" I asked, looking between them. "Both doors were locked."

"We have a master key for every business in town."

I frowned as I digested this tidbit.

"Who else has these master keys?"

"Everyone on the force, plus the fire chief."

I smacked his arm, earning me another menacing look from Doogie Copper.

"Did you ever think that's how someone is getting in here? That's got to be it. One of your guys is using their master key to mess with me!"

Jake frowned. "Hmm. No, I can't see that happening."

"Oh yeah, because you cops are above the law. Break into stores, beat your wife, abuse your kids, just go ahead and commit whatever crimes you want and it's all okay because you have to protect your brothers in blue. You're all the same."

Jake was looking at me thoughtfully, as if my diatribe was giving him an important clue about me. I glared at him.

The other cop cleared his throat. "Chief?"

Jake turned to him, as if he'd forgotten he was there.

"Johnston, go back to the station and do an audit of the master keys, including the ones assigned to the fire station. Let's see if there are any keys missing. I want every key accounted for."

"You got it, Chief."

The kid shot me another warning look and I raised my eyebrows at him, giving him my best "fuck off" look. The hardening of his face told me he'd gotten the message.

The minute the kid locked the door behind him, Jake was on me again.

"You are the most stubborn, foolhardy woman I've ever met," he growled, stalking towards me with a face like a thunder cloud.

I stepped back out of self-preservation. I was pretty sure he wouldn't hurt me, but his expression made me nervous nonetheless. My back hit the wall three steps in. Jake kept coming, crowding close to me as he flattened his hands on the wall on either side of my head.

"What are you doing?" I snapped, raising my chin to meet his gaze. His eyes were dark with anger and something that looked a lot like passion.

"This."

This kiss was just as angry as the first one. I nipped at his lip and this time I was the one shoving my tongue into his mouth. We fought for control, the kiss hot and angry. My heart was thundering in my chest, every nerve in my body on fire.

Jake ran his hands down my arms, grabbing my wrists and pulling them above my head. It was hot as hell, and equally annoying.

"Hey!" I said, my voice way breathier than I would have liked it to be as I broke the kiss to give him a piece of my mind.

Holding my hands immobile over my head with one hand gripping both my wrists, Jake pressed his big body against mine, pinning me to the wall. My breasts were achy against the pressure of his chest, and I could feel an impressive erection against my stomach.

"You're a goddamned menace," he growled against my lips.

"Oh yeah? What are you going to do about it?"

I couldn't decide whether I was crazy or smart to bait him. He kissed me again, his free hand sliding between us to breach the waistband of the yoga pants I wore. He slid his hand into my panties, fingers sliding between my lower lips. He moved his fingers through my wetness a few times and I couldn't help but moan. It felt so good. Jake broke away with a satisfied smirk.

"For someone who hates me so much, you're pretty wet for me."

He rolled his hips against me, and I leaned forward and bit his ear, making him yelp.

"Why don't you shut up and fuck me?" I demanded.

His eyes blazed and he released my hands to shove my yoga pants and underwear down my legs. I kicked them to the side while unzipping his jeans. I was good at multitasking and right now, I'd never been so thankful. Jake shoved his jeans and boxers down to his thighs, releasing his monster cock. He was a big guy, and everything was proportionate. I gripped his dick and squeezed hard enough to make him growl at me.

"Hold on."

Before I knew what he was talking about, he gripped both of my thighs, pulling them around his waist and boosting me up against the wall. I swear I almost came on the spot. I wasn't fat, but I definitely wasn't a small woman. No one had ever boosted me against the wall like that. No one had ever kissed me like this before either, like he couldn't get enough of me. I gripped his shoulders just as he speared me with his cock, impaling me against the wall with one long stroke.

We both paused, and I took a deep breath, trying to relax my internal muscles that were stretched wider than they ever had been before.

Jake lowered his head and kissed me deeply as he started pounding into me. Never one to be passive, I rolled my hips and slammed my pelvis against him with every stroke. It was hard, rough, and dirty, and

I wouldn't have been surprised if Jake fucked me right through the drywall.

He broke away from my mouth, nudging my shirt to the side and nipping his way down to the top of my shoulder. I slid my hands under his tee-shirt, scoring his back with my nails as he bit down on my shoulder hard and sucked the skin into his mouth, marking me.

Jake giving me a hickey like a teenage boy should have pissed me off, but it didn't. For the first time in my entire life, I came without any clitoral stimulation.

I banged my head against the wall as my orgasm crashed through my body. Meanwhile Jake's strokes became erratic. He stiffened against me, then came with a grunt as he pumped into me one, two, three times, filling me with his seed. He dropped his head on my shoulder, panting as we both recovered.

As my heartrate slowed, my common sense returned. What the hell was I doing? Sure, this was the best sex I'd had in my life, but that didn't make this right.

"Let me down," I said, pushing against his shoulders.

Still breathing heavily, Jake stepped back enough for me to drop my feet to the floor and move away from him. He stood there staring at the wall in some kind of fugue state while I found my underwear and tights and pulled them back on. I had no recollection of kicking off my shoes, but I found my Nikes off to the side of where Jake was still standing.

He turned around slowly, and our eyes met and held.

"I'm so..."

I held up my hand.

"Don't say it. We were both here, we are both responsible. It was my idea as much as yours."

Although with my common sense returning quickly, I was having a tough time remembering why I thought this was a good idea. I didn't even like this guy. Jake shoved his impressive dick into his pants and zipped up. Pity. Suddenly his expression changed from shock to alarm.

"Um, Evie. We didn't use a condom. I'm so sorry, I got caught up in the moment and didn't even think of it."

I shrugged. At my age, it didn't matter the way it did when I was younger.

"Neither did I. But I'm in menopause so there's no way you knocked me up if that's what you're worried about. Also, I'm clean. I haven't, um, dated in a while."

One of the many benefits of menopause, in my opinion, was not living in fear that an accident or a broken condom would result in pregnancy. Not having a monthly visitor was also a huge plus.

Jake's expression cleared at my words, but he still looked as shocked as I felt. What had just happened? We were both in our fifties, and we were having crazy hot sex against a wall like kids half our age.

"I am too. Clean, I mean."

He seemed a little discombobulated, and honestly I was glad I wasn't the only one. I'd never seen Jake be anything but confident.

"Okay then, let's just chalk this up to an adrenaline-fueled hate fuck and move on with our lives like it never happened," I suggested. "If I see you in town, I'll just walk the other way."

He strode over to me and placed his big hands on my shoulders, the same way he'd done earlier, although he was calmer now that he wasn't recovering from a shot to the chest with a paintball pellet.

"That was no hate fuck, sweetheart," he said softly, his voice certain.

He pulled me in for a hug, wrapping his arms around me and weak woman that I was, I allowed myself to relax into his warmth for a long moment. For an alpha cop, he gave good hugs. It had been years since I'd had a good hug, and honestly it was almost as good as the sex. Something about Jake made me feel comfortable and safe, and I didn't want to analyze that too closely. I'd worked too hard to be independent.

"If it wasn't a hate fuck, what exactly was that?" I couldn't resist asking.

"The beginning of a beautiful relationship."

Jake

I can't say I was surprised when Evie pushed away from me like I'd slapped her. If there was one thing I'd learned about Evie so far, it was that nothing with her would be easy. She was stubborn and independent and while I admired both of those things about her, it didn't make things easy for me.

"I don't want a relationship," she hissed. "You don't have to date everyone you fuck, you know."

"What's the problem Evie? We're both single, and I bet we have a lot in common."

"No, we don't," she snapped. "But even if we did, I told you, I don't do relationships. And I don't date cops. Ever."

I resisted the urge to push, to demand she tell me what her issue was with cops, or better yet, to throw her over my shoulder and take her home and handcuff her to my bed until she realized that despite our differences, we were perfect for each other. I resisted because I didn't want to push her away, and I was sure that Evie's feelings about what happened between us were just as jumbled as mine were. What had happened between us was life-changing and as sure as I was about her, I was still the tiniest bit freaked out about it. So, I couldn't blame Evie for feeling the same way. Not really.

"Okay, let me walk you to your car and I'll get out of here. We can talk later."

"I'm sleeping here." She pointed to the loft area where she had a little café. "I brought a sleeping bag."

"And your paintball rifle."

She rolled her eyes. "Yeah."

"Okay well, if you're sleeping over here, so am I."

I started towards the stairs, and she ran past me, turning to block my way.

"You're not welcome here, Jake."

I resisted pointing out that I was welcome enough when I fucked her. There was no way I wanted to get shot again. Those paintball shots hurt more than I thought they would.

"Look, it's highly unlikely your vandal is coming back tonight, not after there's been all this ruckus. I'll ask Johnston to come by every hour just in case, and you can relax in a bed instead of sleeping on the hard floor."

Just when I thought I was going to have to throw her over my shoulder and carry her out of here after all, she relented.

"Fine. I just need to get my bag."

I waited downstairs while she went to get her stuff. She returned a few minutes later with a tote bag over her shoulder and a sleeping bag in her hand. We walked through the store together, turning off lights and checking that both doors were locked, not that it mattered. I was pretty sure Evie was right. Someone had a master key. It was the only explanation for why changing the locks hadn't kept them out.

After walking Evie to her car two blocks away, I headed home, suddenly exhausted. It was almost two a.m. and I needed to be on duty at nine. I set my alarm and collapsed on the bed, fully clothed. My last thought before I fell asleep was of Evie.

***

"We've got a big problem."

The next morning, Assistant Chief of Police Elaine Potter came into my office before I even took a sip of my coffee. She was a good officer who shared my philosophy on policing, and we worked together well.

"What is it, Potter?"

"I doubled checked Johnston's work this morning to confirm it, but you were right, we seem to be missing a master key from the station."

"How could that happen?" I asked.

We made officers check those keys in and out with the same procedures we used to give them squad car keys, service revolvers, and badges.

"A number of years ago we had a dirty cop. Name of Brian Peterson. We busted him extorting money from the local business owners, supposedly for extra police protection." She made air quotes for that last part.

I shook my head in disgust. I hated cops who abused their power like that. Potter's face showed the same disgust as mine.

"We confiscated his weapon and badge when we arrested him, but according to the report, he said he'd lost the master key that had been assigned to him. Looks like it was never followed up on since he went to prison, I don't know why. It's the only key unaccounted for."

"Let me guess, Peterson is out now."

Potter nodded. "Released about a month ago, currently on parole. But there's more, Chief."

I raised my eyebrows.

"His parents were the former owners of the bookstore. I gave them a call at their home in Florida this morning to ask about his whereabouts, but they weren't sure where he ended up. They said the last time they talked to him in prison a couple years ago, they had a big fight. The guy was angry that his parents sold the bookstore, claimed he wanted to continue their legacy or something. Of course they didn't buy it, because he never expressed interest in the store before. Told him it was too late anyway, because they'd already sold the business to Ms. Fontenot. He cussed them out and made a bunch of threats, and they told him not to contact them again. The Petersons were a nice couple, but they ended up with a jerk for a son."

Potter took a deep breath and continued her report.

"A few weeks ago, they got an email from him out of the blue, saying he was on parole and was going to go straight and run his own business. They never responded to him. I'm guessing Evie's is the business he wants to run. Although it doesn't look like he has any assets from what I can see, so I'm not sure how he thinks he can take over the store."

"Well, that explains why there are messages telling her to leave, but no major damage to the store," I said. "Although vandalism and vague threats to leave aren't exactly the work of a criminal mastermind.

Potter nodded. "Yeah, that guy was never the brightest bulb on the Christmas tree. Even still, I think we should keep an eye on Evie until we can bring Peterson in. He might get bolder now that he's not been successful in getting her to give up the business with vandalism and vague threats."

"Agreed. And we need to get everything re-keyed right away."

I grimaced, thinking that rekeying all the businesses was going to be a big hit on the police department's very small budget.

"Already on it, Chief. We got the locksmith on hold, waiting for your go-ahead."

"Do it."

I stood up from my desk, unconsciously rubbing the bruise on my chest. Potter smirked.

"Heard Ms. Fontenot tagged you right over the heart with a paint gun last night, thinking you were an intruder."

"You heard right," I admitted, feeling a flush of embarrassment climb my face. "I let her get the drop on me like an amateur. I'm going to go over to her place and let her know what we found out, and work on a safety plan."

"She's a beautiful woman," Potter remarked. "Sweet too. I also heard you two were a bit cozy last night. Johnston said there was a vibe, and your handprint was on her shoulder."

"I'm surprised at you, Potter. I didn't think that you were one to gossip."

My assistant chief looked embarrassed.

"I was raised here, Chief. Gossip is in my DNA, but I usually try to rein it in."

"Good plan. See you later."

I drove over to Evie's house in my cruiser, wondering if I'd find her at home. I wondered why she worked six days a week. From what I'd heard, she was doing really well at the bookstore. She could probably hire an assistant manager or something so she could work less. I should suggest that to her. But maybe not when her paintball gun was around.

Evie wasn't home so I pulled up her phone number and sent her a text.

Jake: *This is Jake. Where are you?*
Evie: *Jake who?*
Jake: *Haha. Seriously I need to talk to you.*
Evie: *How did you get my number?*
Jake: *Police database. What are you doing right now?*
Evie: *I'm busy doing things that are none of your business.*
Jake: *It's about the case. We have a suspect identified.*
Evie: *No way. Color me shocked. Where are you? I'll come now.*
Jake: *I'll meet you at your house.*

Ten minutes later Evie pulled into her driveway. She was loaded down with shopping bags full of groceries.

"Let me help."

"I'm fine," she said stubbornly.

I ignored her, taking the bulk of the bags from her trunk, and following her into her house. It was a cute little cottage style house, about six blocks from the beach. The yard was neat, the grass freshly cut. Inside she'd decorated in mostly whites and dark blue colors, with the occasional pop of red. It was comfortable and cozy and a little quirky, just like Evie herself.

I remembered Marci saying that the only thing Evie got out of the divorce was the house and wondered if she'd lived here with her husband. I couldn't resist asking as I trailed her to the kitchen.

"When did you buy this house?"

She frowned over her shoulder. "Five years ago, after my divorce. Why?"

"Just curious."

We entered the kitchen, which was small but bright, decorated in shades of yellow and dark green. I set the groceries down on the kitchen counter, glancing at a picture on the refrigerator. A younger Evie sat on the beach, a little girl standing between her legs as they both smiled for the camera. They were both wearing swimsuits and sunglasses.

"Your daughter?" I guessed. I wasn't a cop for nothing.

"Yeah, that's Nicole. I think she's about five there."

"It's a great picture. How old is she now?"

"Twenty-seven. She lives in Charleston. She's a social worker."

I could tell by Evie's face that she was proud of her daughter.

"What about you?" she asked curiously. "Do you have kids?"

I shook my head even as my heart warmed at her asking me a personal question.

"No, I was never married."

"You don't have to be married to have kids."

"Oh, I know. But I was in the military for twenty years, and I saw how hard that was on marriages, so I stayed single and always kept everything wrapped up. I was religious about contraception my entire life."

"Until last night," she reminded me.

Just the thought of it had me half-hard. I wanted nothing more than to push Evie down over the counter and fuck her from behind, but I was on duty. I had a job to do, so I moved farther away from her and put the kitchen island between us.

"You said you had news for me?" she asked.

"Yeah. Do you know of a former cop named Brian Peterson?"

She wrinkled her forehead, no doubt trying to interpret my question.

"Of course. He was the Peterson's kid. Those were the people who owned the bookstore before me," she clarified.

"He was always a shithead. Getting into trouble, scamming people. We were all shocked when he went to the police academy and got a job in town here. Everyone hoped that meant he'd grown up, was going to do something useful with his life, especially his poor parents. Then he got busted for running some kind of scam, asking business owners for money for enhanced police protection. To my complete shock, your guys actually arrested him and sent him away."

"Why were you shocked?" I asked curiously. "He broke the law. That's kind of a big part of our job – arresting people who break the law."

"You know how you all are, always protecting your brothers in blue no matter what they do or what laws they break."

She had a look on her face I couldn't interpret. It was a mixture of bitterness and resignation.

"That's the second time you've implied that all cops are dirty."

She raised her eyebrows at me.

"Aren't they?"

"No, they're not," I growled. "In fact—."

"Why did you ask about Brian?" she interrupted before I could say more.

"We followed up on your idea that there was a missing master key. Turns out Brian Peterson never turned his into the station when he was arrested. Claimed he lost it. Coincidentally, he was paroled about a week before your first break-in."

"Why would Brian mess with my store?" she asked in confusion.

"We talked to the Petersons. When he heard his parents were retiring, he asked them to cancel the sale and hold the store until he was paroled, but they refused. Apparently he was furious that they sold his legacy."

She laughed. It was the first time I'd heard her laugh and the sound was sweet.

"His legacy? That kid never worked at the store unless his parents forced him. Mrs. Peterson caught him stealing from the till several times and finally they just gave up on him ever taking over for them. He was always getting into trouble. It was so bad they kicked him out of the house the minute he turned eighteen. He was a total jackass, and the Petersons were such a sweet couple, it totally broke their heart."

"Well, he's a jackass on the loose, with a key to your store and every other business in town. I'm increasing patrols at the store and around your house, but until we catch him, you're going to need to be careful and watch your six. We have no idea what he might do as he gets increasingly frustrated."

"Okay. I'll keep my eyes out."

"And no more playing vigilante in your store."

Evie stalked over to me and poked me in the chest with her pointer finger. I don't think she did it on purpose, but she managed to poke me right where I had the bruise from the paintball shot. I bit my lip to keep from grimacing. I had a manly reputation to protect.

"You listen here Jake Wilson. You are not the boss of me. I'm a grown woman, and I'll do what I want, when I want. You don't get to come over here and stand in my own damn house and tell me what to do."

I grabbed her hand and used the leverage to pull her between my legs, my other hand coming to the back of her neck.

"Well, that's where you're wrong."

Evie

I opened my mouth to give Jake a piece of my mind, but he kissed me before I could even get a word out. Damn him. The man had magic lips. I'd been with a fair number of men over my life, and never had anyone been able to kiss me senseless. Literally. When Jake touched me, everything in my head quieted, my focus solely on how he made me feel.

It really pissed me off.

Jake's kiss was claiming, his hand on my neck dominating. I wished I didn't like it as much as I did. Normally I liked to be the one in control, but something in me thrilled at Jake's dominance even as I fought it. I'd been up most of the night reliving our little interlude in the store. I'd even dreamed about it.

Suddenly he stood up and lifted me to sit on the kitchen island, all in one smooth move.

"What are you doing?" I asked, hating the breathless quality of my voice.

"I've been dying to get a taste of you since we first met."

His brown eyes met mine and I'm pretty sure my panties disintegrated from the rush of heat that flooded my core.

He placed one big hand on my sternum, gently pushing me down until I was laying across the counter. In the space of a minute, he'd pulled off my capris and underwear, and sat back down on the stool, shifting my legs over his shoulders. I was never a small woman, and there was a part of me that really enjoyed how easily he could move me around.

Leaning forward, Jake ran his tongue up my slit. The touch of his tongue was enough to make me want to levitate off the counter. He used one large hand to hold my hip down, then began eating me out in earnest. I was already impossibly wet just from sparring with him and kissing him, and the sound of Jake lapping up my essence was obscenely loud in my otherwise quiet kitchen.

I was well and truly ramped up when he suddenly slid one thick finger into my channel. I made a keening sound as he began pushing his finger in and out, then added a second finger. His tongue homed in on my clit, circling the swollen bundle of nerves with rough strokes. I dug my fingers into the short strands of his hair, pressing his face closer against my needy pussy, directing him to where I needed him the most.

Suddenly Jake bent his fingers, finding my G-spot, and that was it for me. I spasmed beneath him, my mouth opening in a silent scream as wave after wave of pleasure raced through me. Jake slowed his rough motions, easing me down as aftershocks wrung me out and left me boneless and panting on the counter.

I looked up as Jake slid back from me, his lips wet with my essence, his face full of masculine satisfaction. He stood up, easing my feet onto the chair he'd just vacated, and I pushed myself up on my elbows. Jake was sporting an impressive erection, and I assumed he'd be opening his zipper for round two. Instead, he stepped back.

"What are you doing?" I asked in confusion. I wasn't used to guys going down on me just for funsies and not wanting something in return. Then again, Jake wasn't like any other guy that I'd been with.

"I'm on duty. I need to get back to work."

My mouth opened and I struggled to sit up.

"What about you?" I asked, pointing vaguely towards his crotch where an impressive erection strained the fabric.

"I'm good."

My eyebrows rose in shock.

"You're just going to leave?"

I damn near bit off my tongue as those needy words escaped my mouth. Damn Jake and his magic lips, making me want nothing more than for him to fuck me until we were both exhausted.

Getting a hold of myself, I hopped off the counter on unsteady legs, finding my clothes and pulling them on as he watched with a tiny smirk. I wished I had my paintball rifle close by so I could shoot him again.

"I've increased patrols around the store and added your house to our patrol route," he repeated the same thing he'd told me earlier. Maybe he wasn't as unaffected by what just happened as he pretended he was.

"Be careful until we bring this guy in. You've got my cell number, call me if anything happens. Don't take any more unnecessary chances," he ordered in his stern cop voice.

"*Don't take any more unnecessary chances,*" I mimicked him. "*Let the big strong man protect you.*"

Jake frowned at me.

"Protecting people is my job."

I waved him off. "Yeah. Okay. Well, thanks for the orgasm. You can go now."

I couldn't decide what I was more angry about. Getting me off and not moving to round two, or the domineering way he was talking to me. Maybe both.

By the time Jake pulled away from the house, I'd worked up a good mad. And I knew what could help: deep cleaning the house and hanging out with my girls. Emma, Dawn, and I had been friends for over twenty-five years. They knew me better than anyone, and I wanted to process everything that had happened with Jake with the only people who truly understood me.

Evie: *Are you two available tonight? I need some girl time.*

Dawn: *The restaurant is closed on Mondays, so I'm in.*

Emma: *I'll let Wyatt know I have plans. What are we doing?*

Evie: *Margaritas at Jose's?*

Dawn: *Sounds great.*

Emma: *Let's meet at six and get dinner to line our stomachs.*

Evie: *Yay. I need all the margaritas after the last 24 hours. See you all then.*

***

I squinted against the bright sun coming in the windows. Had I forgotten to close the curtains last night? I opened one eye. Wait. Where was I? And what the hell had I eaten? My mouth tasted like a dead animal.

Feeling someone shift behind me, I looked down and saw one large arm wrapped around my waist. What the hell? I slid my hand beneath the blanket. I was wearing my shirt and underwear, but no pants.

I tried to subtly shift out from underneath the arm, but it tightened against me.

"Relax," a sleepy voice instructed. "We don't have to be up for a while."

Oh crap. I recognized that voice. Jake. What the hell was I doing in his bed with him? I swear I'd promised myself to never let that asshole touch me again after what happened in my kitchen.

"I have to pee," I croaked. The arm loosened and I slid out of the bed and headed into the en-suite bathroom. I sat on the toilet and noticed that Jake had left a new toothbrush and towel on the counter for me. That was incredibly sweet, but I still wasn't sure what happened.

I stood up and groaned, the movement jarring my throbbing head.

I felt marginally better after washing my face and brushing my teeth. When I came out of the bathroom, Jake was sitting on the bed wearing only boxers. I grimaced as I noticed the large purple-yellow bruise on his pec from where I'd nailed him with the paintball gun. He looked rumpled and sleepy and hot as hell. He held out a large glass of water and a bottle of ibuprofen.

"Here. Drink."

I shook out some pills and swallowed them down, drinking the glass of water in one gulp. My mouth was dry as the Sahara.

Standing felt like a lot of effort, so I dropped into the armchair across from the bed. It was one of those big, overstuffed chairs, perfect for reading. I glanced at the table and saw a stack of manly magazines, but no books. Did the guy not own a book? No wonder I'd never seen him in the store before the vandalism happened. It was just more proof of how incompatible we were.

"What happened last night?" I finally asked. "Why am I here? And did we—?"

I raised one eyebrow and nodded towards the bed, but Jake shook his head.

"Of course not. You were too drunk. I didn't want to take advantage of you. But I have to say, you get kind of handsy when you're drunk."

An image of me trying to kiss Jake while he helped me into bed flashed in my mind. Ugh, I was pretty sure I'd grabbed his dick too. I squeezed my eyes shut, willing the memories to return from the drunken recesses of my mind. I remembered going to Jose's with my two best friends and telling them everything that had happened with Jake. I remembered ordering a pitcher of margaritas with our chips and salsa, and another one with dinner. After that things got a little blurry.

"Do you remember leaving the restaurant last night?" he asked. "I understand you were there for a few hours, drinking."

I shook my head. "It's all a blur."

"Johnston called me around ten thirty last night. He was passing by the bookstore and saw you there. He said that you and two other woman stumbled down the sidewalk and went into your store, while repeatedly yelling, 'Come and get us, Brian!' and spewing profanities. Then the three of you came out brandishing brooms and a mop like weapons and started marching back and forth on the sidewalk in front of the store screaming for Brian to come get you. Johnston threatened to take you all in for drunk and disorderly if you didn't calm down, but then the three of you got belligerent and started threatening him with your brooms, so he called for reinforcements."

"Oh my God," I whispered as it all came rushing back like a movie in my head.

My friends and I didn't drink a lot normally, not at our age, but when we did, we tended to get a tiny bit rambunctious. It was as true now as it had been when we were younger. I remembered all the trouble we'd gotten into when we went to the Florida Keys to celebrate my fiftieth birthday. I needed a new liver after that trip. Although the good thing was that my fuddy-duddy sister Teresa had met her husband on that vacation thanks to us. Like Emma, she'd somehow landed herself a billionaire, and a nice one at that.

"When Reyes got there as back-up, you were yelling at Johnston and calling him 'Doogie Copper.'"

I giggled at that one, and Jake gave me a stern look that made my pussy spasm.

"Reyes apparently knows one of your friends, the one who's a nurse..."

"Emma."

"Yeah, so he called Emma's boyfriend and Johnston called me. Wyatt and I got there at the same time. He and I are good friends."

I rolled my eyes. Of course he was friends with Wyatt.

"I knew he was dating someone, but I didn't realize it was a friend of yours. Anyway, Wyatt volunteered to take Emma and Dawn home with him, and I said I'd take you with me and keep an eye on you."

"Gee thanks," I said drily.

"Then I drove you here, you projectile vomited into my bushes, and I put you to bed."

I had a memory of myself hurling into the bushes while Jake held my hair back. Well that explained the horrible taste in my mouth this morning. I'm glad Jake had left me a toothbrush.

"Oh Lord, it's all coming back to me now. Thank you for taking care of me. And I apologize about your bushes," I said grudgingly.

Jake shrugged.

"Nothing I couldn't rinse off with a hose. But there's something else."

I looked up nervously. "What?"

The smirk was back.

"You told me that you really like me."

"I did not."

He nodded. "You did. In fact, your exact words were, 'Don't tell Jake, but I like him. I really like him. He's hot as fuck.' And then you passed out."

I lowered my head into my hands, squeezing against my skull as if that would help everything be better. It didn't work.

"Can you take me home now please?" I asked in a small voice.

"How about we go out to breakfast?" he countered. "You need greasy breakfast food to help with your hangover."

It was a testament to how shitty I felt that I didn't argue.

Jake

Evie and I had a quick and mostly quiet breakfast at the local diner, then I dropped her off at her house and headed into the station. She looked much better after eating. I tried to convince her to have dinner with me after she closed the shop, but once again she shot me down. I reminded myself to be patient and give her time to come around, but it was getting harder and harder. Now that I'd tasted her, I only wanted her more.

As I drove back through town, I tried to puzzle out what was going on with the two of us. It was clear to me that I loved her, that I had loved her since the moment I laid eyes on her, but she was also the most stubborn and frustrating woman I'd ever dated.

If we could call what we were doing dating. I guessed one hate fuck and eating her out on the counter didn't really make a relationship. The attraction between us was nothing short of explosive. And waking up with her in my arms had been incredible, despite her grumpy disposition. I wanted to do it again every morning for the rest of my life. But I was at a loss on how to move forward with her and break down her walls.

What I hadn't told her is what else she said to me last night. After telling me that she liked me, she'd added, "It's too bad Jake's a damn cop or I would totally fall for him."

I'd asked her to tell me why she hated cops, but she passed out before I could get any more information. Clearly she'd had a bad experience with a cop before, but without knowing what happened, it was hard to put her mind at ease. I wondered what it would take to get her to open up to me.

My cell phone buzzed later that morning with a message from Wyatt. The billionaire and I met when I was helping him with a security issue not long after I became police chief. We'd clicked and become fast friends, often getting together to grab a beer or watch sports. I hadn't seen as much of him the last two months since he'd fallen in love with his nurse, Emma, after having an emergency appendectomy.

Wyatt: *How about meeting for a drink tonight?*
Jake: *I'm off at seven.*
Wyatt: *I'll meet you at our usual place at seven-thirty.*

When I got to the bar, Wyatt was already there, an open stool by his side. We shook hands and I ordered a beer.

"How were your drunken patients?" I asked him.

Wyatt chuckled. "They both felt better after they puked. I told them they are too old to be drinking like that."

"What did they say?"

"Emma told me to fuck off and Dawn gave me the finger without lifting her head off my kitchen table."

I laughed. "Sounds like you have your hands full with that girlfriend of yours."

"I was going to say the same thing to you, man."

I groaned, remembering how I'd had to carry Evie away last night as she flailed around with her broom, screeching, and swearing.

"Yeah, Evie seems to hate me, except sometimes she doesn't. She's it for me, I'm totally in love with her, but she so independent and prickly, it's getting frustrating. I think it has at least something to do with my job, because she keeps telling me she doesn't date cops."

"Did she tell you her father was a cop?"

My head swung his way. Evie had told me next to nothing about herself, probably because we were usually fighting. "No."

Wyatt took a drink of his beer, his expression thoughtful.

"I probably shouldn't tell you this, but I overheard Emma and Dawn talking this morning. They were debating about whether Evie hated you as much as she says she does, or if she's just trying to hide how much she's into you."

"She's hiding it pretty well," I said miserably.

"Then Dawn said that no matter how much she likes you, Evie could never be in a relationship with a cop, after the way her father was so abusive to his wife and kids. It's a hard line for her."

My blood ran cold. "Her father abused her?"

"I asked Emma about it later. She said he was a cop with a penchant for violence, and the local cops protected him because he was one of their own. Never arrested him, no matter how much he knocked around his wife. It took the mother years to get away, and by then Evie was out of the house and on her own."

Suddenly Evie's comments about dirty cops were making more sense.

"Anyway, Emma would kill me if she knew I was telling you this, but I saw the way you were looking at her last night and...I see now that I'm not the only one who's found love."

"Yeah, but Emma didn't actively hate you when you got together."

"No. But she didn't trust me, and my having money was not a point in my favor with that one. If I'd had any doubts about her character, her complete disinterest in my money dispelled them."

He took another sip of beer and smirked.

"Now she's totally into me. I can't wait to marry her."

"You're getting married already?" I said louder than I probably should.

Wyatt shushed me. "I'm waiting a while to ask her. Emma's like a deer, you have to approach her gently, with no fast movements."

"If Emma is a deer, Evie is a feral cat."

Wyatt laughed. "You're not wrong about that one, my friend. But it sounds like she cares more than she lets on, based on what I overheard from Dawn and Emma."

When I finished with Wyatt, I headed home. I was tempted to go over to Evie's, but I figured she needed space. I settled on the couch to watch some ESPN. The phone woke me up just before midnight. Somehow I wasn't surprised that it was Johnston.

"Chief?" Johnston's voice was wary, like he was expecting me to be mad.

"What did she do now?" I asked, knowing this had to be about Evie.

"Um, you'd better come to the bookstore. You need to see this for yourself."

For the second time in a week, I grabbed my shoes and service weapon and raced over to Boozy Books in the middle of the night.

All the lights were on in the shop, with Johnston standing guard by the open door.

"Status report," I barked at him.

He stepped aside with a grimace.

"I was doing my patrol and I found this."

I stepped into the store and stopped in my tracks. Evie, Emma, and Dawn were all there, surrounding a blonde man who was sitting on the floor, immobilized by duct-tape wrapped around him from his ankles to his knees. His arms were taped to his body, and another strip of duct tape covered his mouth. The man looked furious. I recognized him from the mugshots as Brian Peterson. Officer Reyes stood close by, his eyes pinned to the group as if expecting more trouble.

Evie held her paintball rifle, pointing it at the man's head. The large splatters of paint on Peterson's chest, abdomen, and thigh told me that Evie had gotten several good shots off the guy. Dawn held a broom, brandishing it like a weapon, while Emma was recording everything on her phone. I had a bad feeling I'd be seeing this on the town's Facebook page within a few hours.

"What the ever-loving fuck is going on here?" I bellowed.

Evie jumped, turning to face me with a defiant glare. "We did what the police couldn't. We captured Brian Peterson."

"Caught him in the act too," Dawn said, pointing to a large knife and a can of spray paint several feet away on the floor.

I rubbed my temples.

"Can someone start from the beginning please?"

"You're never going to believe this," Reyes muttered.

"The girls and I were standing guard," Evie began. "We figured he was coming in the back door, to avoid anyone seeing him through the front windows, so we slicked up the floor by the door with oil."

She pointed behind her and I had flashes of that movie where the parents left the kid home alone to fight burglars.

"When we heard the door squeak, we got into position. Brian here crept in like the lowlife scum he is, and as we planned, he slipped on the oil like a cartoon character with a banana peel." Her mouth quirked. "Then we covered him with a fishing net."

That explained the large net on the floor next to the puddle of what looked like cooking oil.

"I can't believe this worked," Reyes added, shaking his head. "These ladies are straight up crazy."

Evie shot him a look that was so venomous I felt my balls crawl up into my body.

"He managed to get out of the net before we could restrain him, so I shot him a few times with the paint ball gun. He fell on the floor, stunned. Then we all sat on him to keep him still while we duct taped his hands and legs to secure him until you guys could arrest him."

"Then he called us cunts, so we duct taped his damn mouth," Dawn added, proudly.

"Well Brian, I guess you would have gotten away with it if it hadn't been for these meddling kids."

Evie gave me a look of shock. "Did you just make a joke? And a Scooby Doo reference? I didn't know you had it in you."

I pointed at her and gave her my best glower. "You're going to need to be quiet, or I'm arresting all of you for obstruction of justice."

"Obstruction?" she scoffed. "I think what you mean to say is, thank you for solving my case for me."

That was it. I was done. Clearly Evie had no concern about her personal safety. My heart pounded as I thought of all the things that could have happened while they were playing detective. A trained cop and felon against three middle-aged women? I couldn't believe no one had been hurt. If I had lost her...

I looked at Johnston and Reyes.

"Can you handle this?" I asked. "Lock him up and then get these ladies home."

"Yes sir," they answered in unison.

I grabbed Evie's wrist.

"You're coming with me."

Evie

Jake tugged me out of the store by the wrist. I planted my feet when we hit the sidewalk.

"Jake! What the hell are you doing?"

His voice was eerily calm.

"You've got two choices. Come with me voluntarily, or I throw you over my shoulder and cuff you to my car."

"Handcuffs? I had no idea you were so kinky, Chief." I replied saucily.

If Jake were a cartoon, there would have been smoke coming out of his ears. He moved closer and I could see the intent in his eyes.

"Fine, fine, I'll come with you," I said petulantly. "But for the record, it's under duress."

He handed me into his car – the front seat at least, not the prisoner section – and drove to his house without saying a single word. I glanced over at him, noting the muscle that was twitching over his jaw. I'd never seen him this mad before.

"Jake..."

He held up a finger.

"Not a word Evie. I'm hanging onto my temper here by the thinnest of threads."

I sighed and crossed my arms, getting up my own head of steam the farther we got away from the store. I was proud of the way my girls and I were able to catch Brian tonight, and I could already tell that I was in for a lecture from Mr. "I'm the Law Here". I didn't like it.

Jake pulled into his driveway, then opened my door, pulling me out. His touch was gentle, but firm. He tugged me into the kitchen, pointing to a chair. I sat down without a word and watched as he grabbed a bottle of whiskey off the top of the refrigerator. He poured two healthy shots and slid one to me. I ignored it as he downed his shot, then poured himself a second one and drank that one too.

Taking a deep breath, Jake leaned forward, his hands flat on the table. "What. The. Fuck. Were you thinking?"

I raised an eyebrow at the deceptively calm tone, completely at odds with his words.

"I was thinking someone was fucking with my store, with my livelihood, and I wasn't going to sit on my hands waiting for your guys to figure it out. Also, I was thinking I was an adult, on my own property, and could do what the hell I wanted."

"Brian is a criminal who's had law enforcement training. He could have easily overpowered you three and hurt you. He could have stabbed you or shot you."

"But he didn't," I pointed out. "We got the drop on him and solved the case. So again...you're welcome for doing your job for you."

I watched in fascination as a red flush climbed up Jake's face. I wondered if he had high blood pressure. I hoped not, because he looked like he was about to stroke out. He looked up at the ceiling, as if seeking inspiration from the heavens.

After several deep breaths, he met my gaze. His voice was ragged but serious.

"I love you, Evie. Don't you get it? If something had happened to you tonight, I don't know what I would've done. It would have killed me."

I ignored the warm flush in my chest and instead said, "You can't love me. We've known each other for two weeks."

"When you know, you know."

"Look Jake, I'm sure you're a nice guy. And I admit I'm attracted to you and the sex, well, we both know that was off the charts. But I'm not looking for anything serious, and I'm definitely not interested in dating a cop."

I looked down at my hands and added in a soft voice. "I'm sorry. Truly I am."

"You don't want to date me because of what happened with your father? Is that it?"

My head snapped up so fast I think I sprained a muscle. "How...?"

My mind raced. Only two people knew my history: Dawn and Emma. I connected the dots between Emma to Wyatt to Jake and felt a rush of irritation.

"Damn that Emma."

"It's not her fault. Wyatt overheard her and Dawn talking about it. She didn't intentionally betray your confidence."

When I didn't respond, Jake reached across the battered wooden table and took my hand. It was warm and calloused and I didn't want to think too hard about why everything in me once again calmed with his touch.

"Not every cop is dirty," Jake said softly.

"Tell that to the guy I hit with a paint gun tonight."

"About that. Who taught you to shoot?"

I rolled my eyes. "My father, of course. It might have been the only decent thing he ever did."

"Evie, I know you're scared. I know you need time. All I'm asking is that you look past your father and see me for who I really am. Get to know me better. I've never felt like this before, this, this, whatever this is between us. And I think it's the same for you. Please, just give me a chance. Give us a chance."

Damned if I didn't want to do exactly what he asked. Maybe it would be okay to meet him halfway. I'd talked about this at length with Emma and Dawn, and they'd made the point that I couldn't assume that all cops were like my father. Jake had done nothing to give me any indication that he was violent. And the fact was, I was totally crazy about him. As much as he annoyed me, I couldn't deny that I also liked him. A lot.

"I guess we could try dating, and see how that goes," I responded.

Jake looked as surprised as I felt.

I rushed to add, "But I make no guarantees."

Jake studied my face for a long moment, then nodded.

"Okay. That's good enough for now. We can talk more later. It's been a big night, let's go to bed."

"Is there an invitation in there somewhere? Because I believe I've been crystal clear about how I feel about being ordered around."

He took a deep breath.

"Evie Fontenot. Would you please sleep over with me?"

"Since you asked nicely, I guess I will," I said primly.

He stood up and once again grabbed my wrist, leading me towards the bedroom.

"You don't need to drag me everywhere, you know," I told him.

He turned around and before I knew what he was doing, he somehow tossed me over his shoulder. I huffed out a deep breath as my abdomen pressed against his hard shoulder. He gave me a sharp tap on the ass, and I squealed.

"You're going to be the death of me Evie. I just know it."

Jake strode into the bedroom and dumped me on the bed. I watched while he took off everything but his boxers, then slid into bed next to me. I rolled over to look at him in confusion.

"What are you doing?"

"Going to sleep. It's late."

I ran my fingers down the salt and pepper hair that covered his chest. I could tell he was still angry about us taking the law into our own hands, but I knew he'd get over it. I was actually pretty proud of myself and my girls.

"I'm a little keyed up from my adventure. I think I need to do something to calm down."

Before he could answer I moved to straddle his waist and pulled off my shirt and bra. I realized he'd never actually seen the top of me naked before, and hoped he wasn't too disappointed that my large breasts were a bit saggy, and my stomach was soft. I exhaled as I saw his eyes darken with appreciation.

His hands went right to my breasts, teasing the nipples between his fingers. I braced my hands against his hips and arched my back, giving him access. I could feel his cock lengthening next to my ass. Jake jackknifed to sitting and took one nipple into his mouth, teasing the other with his fingers.

Suddenly he pulled back and looked at me with an expression that I couldn't interpret.

"One day Evie, we're going to do this slow and take our time getting to know each other's bodies. However, today is not that day."

He rolled me over to my back and practically ripped my pants and underwear off. His fingers dipped between my lower lips, smirking as he found me dripping wet.

"Is this for me?" he growled.

"Well, it's certainly not for Brian Peterson."

Jake took my hands in his and pinned them to the bed on either side of my head, then shoved his hips between my thighs. I wrapped my legs around his waist as he entered me in one long thrust.

We both groaned in pleasure.

Jake started pumping in and out of me roughly, and I held on tight, lifting my hips to meet him with every stroke. It had never been like this with anyone else, so all-consuming. I was suddenly glad that I'd made the decision to give him a chance. And as my orgasm thundered through my body, I only hoped this would last.

Jake

Evie rolled over with a groan and pressed her face against my shoulder to block out the light. I hugged her tight to me, feeling a wave of happiness. Last night had been incredible. Well, not the part where she could have been killed by an idiot criminal, but the part afterward. I'd loved falling asleep with our bodies wrapped around each other.

Evie groaned, then shifted up to give me a soft kiss on the cheek.

"Good morning."

"Good morning, sunshine. What's on your agenda today?"

"I'm working at the store, and then we have book club tonight."

"Ah yes, the infamous boozy book club." Assistant Chief Potter was an avid participant, as well as several other women on my team, so I'd heard a lot about it and understood the premise. "What's your theme this month?"

She gave me a strange look. "Martinis & Mysteries."

"What's wrong?"

She shook her head.

"Nothing. It's just that last month our theme was Bubbly & Billionaires, and Emma met and fell in love with a billionaire. And this month was Martinis & Mysteries, and I solved a mystery."

"That's a strange coincidence. What's your theme for next month?"

"Bourbon & Bikers. I guess one of us is going to meet a biker," she laughed.

"Not you. You're taken."

She rolled her eyes. "I like possessive about as much as I like bossy. Remember that."

***

It had been two months since my little Nancy Drew and her girl detective friends had solved the mystery of the vandal cop. Brian had gone back to prison on his parole violation and would likely have extra time added to his sentence for breaking and entering and willful destruction of property. I'd had some time to interrogate Peterson before the state marshals took him and had been surprised that his grand plan was to get Evie to close the shop, with no idea how he'd take it over himself. What an idiot. He'd had no money and no plan for what he would do if he'd succeeded in getting Evie to give up the shop.

Since Brian's arrest, Evie and I basically spent every day together. We alternated between sleeping at her place or mine, and I still stopped by the store most mornings to bring her a caramel macchiato. I might have gotten into the sweet coffee drinks myself, though I'd deny it if anyone asked me. When Evie got off work we would either go to dinner, order take-out, or one of us would cook. It was all very homey.

Evie had finally hired an assistant manager for her store, which mean she didn't have to work as many hours as she did before. Although she never said that she did it to give us more time together, I appreciated having more time with her.

Honestly, things between us were going better than I could have dreamed. We still fought, especially when Evie was being stubborn or she thought that I was being high-handed, but the make-up sex was out of this world. She challenged me, in all the best ways.

I'd avoided talking about commitment, trusting my instincts to give her more time to get comfortable with me. She was still independent and stubborn as hell, but she was gradually letting me in, and I was grateful for every hard-won bit of trust she showed me. I'd even met her daughter on a video call last week. That felt like a big step.

Evie padded out of bed, heading for the bathroom. I laid in bed, listening as she brushed her teeth and washed her face. Exiting the bathroom, she headed for her walk-in closet, then walked out a few seconds later with a weird look on her face.

"What's wrong?" I asked, pushing myself to sitting.

"I think you've got more clothes in my closet than I do," she said ruefully. "You're lucky I love you enough to share my closet space."

My eyes widened and Evie clamped her hand over her mouth as she realized what she'd said. I rolled out of bed and walked slowly to where she stood frozen in place.

"What did you say?"

She winced and dropped her hand. "You heard me. Don't make me say it again."

I wrapped my arms over her shoulders and stared at her until she looked up and met my gaze. Her expression turned stubborn, something I'd seen a lot of during our relationship.

"Fine. I love you. Okay?" she said grudgingly. "I hope you're happy."

I whooped, grabbing her waist, and picking her up to twirl her in a circle, her feet flailing.

"Put me down, you idiot. You're going to hurt yourself."

I carried her to the bed and gently laid her on her back, then crawled over her, pinning her to the bed with the lower half of my body. Propping myself up on my elbows, I stared down at her.

"Say it again."

"What's in it for me?" she asked teasingly.

"Lots and lots of orgasms."

She pretended to think. "Okay, I'll accept your offer. I love you Jake, even if you are the most annoying person I know."

"I love you too, Nancy Drew, even though you're the most annoying person I know too."

I lowered my head and kissed her deeply. We didn't get out of bed again for a very long time.

Epilogue – Evie

"Come on, we have to get over to Wyatt's. I promised Emma I'd do her hair."

Emma was marrying her boyfriend Wyatt today and although they'd only been dating for less than a year, I was happy for them. They were the perfect couple. Since Wyatt and Jake were friends, the four of us had double dated several times.

As for me and Jake, things were going great. Last month I'd finally gotten tired of switching off between houses and let him move in with me. We'd been practically living together anyway, so it felt right, especially after I admitted the truth: I was madly in love with him. He was bossy and annoying, but also incredibly thoughtful. And he liked to cook and do laundry. I mean, who was I to let a guy like that get away?

If only Dawn could figure out what she was doing with the guy in her life, the three of us all would be settled...

Jake came out into the living room, looking like everyone's silver fox fantasy in a dark suit, crisp white shirt, and a skinny red tie. He was going to be best man for Wyatt, while Dawn and I were the co-bridesmaids.

My boyfriend looked at my dress, whistling under his breath.

"Damn, you clean up well," he teased.

"You don't look too terrible yourself," I retorted with a laugh. I'd never seen him in a suit before, and I had to admit that I really liked it.

"There's just one thing you need to complete your outfit."

"What's that?" I asked as I slipped into my shoes.

"This."

Jake held out his hand, revealing a dark blue velvet box.

"What's this?" I asked suspiciously.

"Open it and see."

I opened the box, revealing an adorable diamond engagement ring with a silver band. I looked up at Jake, but he'd dropped to one knee. I looked at him in shock while he grabbed my hand.

"Marry me, Evie."

"Is there a question there?" I teased.

To my surprise, I didn't want to throw up at the idea of marrying Jake. In fact, it felt...right.

"Evie Fontenot, love of my life, will you please do me the honor of being my wife?"

I stared at the ring in his hand, and when I didn't answer right away, he added, "You can think about it if you want."

My heart pinched at the look of uncertainty on his face. Jake was definitely the more affectionate and demonstrative of the two of us, and I knew he still struggled to read me sometimes. I wasn't answering because I was trying hard not to burst into tears and ruin my make-up. I'd told myself I would never get married again, but with Jake, it didn't seem so scary. In fact, it seemed...right.

"I don't need to think about it. My answer is yes."

Jake jumped to his feet. "Really?"

"Yes, I will marry you, but on two conditions."

"What?"

"First, I'm not changing my name, so don't even ask me."

"Done."

"And second, you have to promise to not interfere in my work solving mysteries with my girl gang."

Jake laughed. "You're going to keep me on my toes, aren't you?"

"You know it, copper. Now how about we seal the deal with a kiss?"

"That's the best idea you've had yet."

***

Want to hear more about how Evie's friend finally finds love? Be sure to check out my book "Bourbon and Bikers", coming in Fall 2022. Click here[1] to join my mailing list and be the first to know when the book is available.

---

1. https://storyoriginapp.com/giveaways/62ee758e-068f-11eb-904e-c373f6014fe1

Did you like this book? Show the love and leave me a review. Reviews are like puppies, they make you feel happy.

Keep reading for a special excerpt from "Until You Came Along", available everywhere now.

Special Preview

Until You Came Along by Rose Bak

Jen heard the rumbling from all the way in the kitchen. Wiping her hands on a towel, she walked to the front porch to watch the two large buses drive up the long driveway to the farmhouse. Belching smoke, they idled and came to a stop, one behind the other.

Although it wasn't even 10 a.m. yet, the sun shone brightly in the summer sky, showcasing the dust left in the wake of the parked buses. A bird squawked loudly in the sudden silence as a serious looking young woman scurried out of the first bus, glasses askew, a clipboard gripped in one hand, cellphone in another. Two large mountains of men followed her, hulking shadows.

"Jen Oliver? The band is here. We'll just come in and...." she moved to enter the house, but Jen stood her ground, blocking the door.

"Where are they?" she asked the woman, her tone icy. "And who are you exactly?"

The woman looked flustered for a brief moment before her stern mask fell back down again. She shuffled her cell phone into the hand with the clipboard and stuck out her now-free hand to shake. "I'm Simone. I manage the band."

Jen ignored her hand. "Well, manage them out of those buses. They don't get to send the help out to greet their sister."

Simone looked confused as she dropped her hand back to her side. "They're all sleeping. They had a late night. We'll just come in and check...."

"Still up all night and sleeping all day, huh? That's been the same since they were teenagers." Jen shook her head. On the farm they had all been taught the value of hard work – up before dawn, work all day, and early to bed. Somehow those lessons hadn't really stuck with her brothers despite her grandparents' best efforts over the years.

Of course, the boys, as she still thought of them, had been away from the farm for ten years now, chasing fame and fortune as the biggest boy band to hit the charts since N Sync. Like the band that came before them, the Oliver Boys had grown up but continued to enchant teenage girls across the world with their pop tunes.

Simone clearly felt protective of the boys. "They played last night in Wichita you know," she said sternly. "The show went until almost midnight, then they met the fans and press for hours after."

"By meet the fans and press do you mean got drunk and partied?" Jen's tone did little to hide her opinion of the boys and their reputation for debauched partying.

Simone shook her head. "They've mostly settled down now. There's not as much partying as there used to be when they were younger. But they still need to make an effort to meet people, it's part of the job. Now we'll just come in and...."

Jen shook her head. "Well," she drawled. "When they wake up from their so-called job, you send them on in. The rest of you need to find some other place to bunk. I'm not running a hotel for drunken roadies here."

A slight movement behind Simone caught Jen's eyes. One of the giant men flanking Simone shook with repressed laughter, his mouth twisted in a smirk but his face otherwise impassive. Jen looked at him for the first time. He was the size of a small tank, several inches over six feet tall, with impossibly wide shoulders and large biceps. His hair was a dark blond, "dishwater blonde" her grandma would call it, worn military short. He was dressed all in black, and she noticed a gun on the shoulder holster. Jen wondered why he felt he needed a gun out here in the middle of nowhere. She felt him watching her and she raised her eyes to his, a shiver of awareness coursing through her, although she couldn't make out his eyes behind the dark sunglasses.

"Miss Oliver..." Simone started again.

"Jen"

"OK, then, Jen, we need to do a security sweep before the boys come in. If you could just move aside, we'll get started." Simone nodded decisively.

"A security—-what the hell are you talking about?"

Simone turned to the man who'd been staring at Jen earlier. "This is Nick, he's head of security for the band. He'll be doing a security sweep and assessment with Brian here," she pointed at the second silent man.

"We don't need a security sweep. This place is as safe as it comes. We don't even lock the doors in these parts."

Simone shook her head again, vibrating with irritation and clearly not used to people disobeying her orders. "No way. The boys don't go anywhere without a security check ahead of time. I'm afraid I have to insist."

Jen shot her a look filled with venom, her tone as cold as ice. "You can insist all you like but this is my property. You have no right to it, and neither do the boys. Y'all can just run along now, I'm not having some ginormous strangers poking around my property. Don't make me sic the dogs on you." Simone's mouth dropped open.

This was an empty threat. Jen's three dogs looked mean, but they were incurably friendly. They were just as likely to lick a person to death as bite them. Jen had a sneaking suspicion that if someone tried to kill her the dogs would jump over her body and leave with the killer. But these music people didn't need to know that. If there was one thing Jen hated, it was music people. They were way too self-important and proud.

"Excuse me ma'am," the guy called Nick interrupted.

"Jen," she repeated, a trace of irritation in her tone.

He inclined his head. "Sorry. Jen. As Simone mentioned, I'm head of security for the band. We've had some issues and I would be very appreciative if my team could just poke around for a bit and make sure there's nothing amiss." His tone was deferential and charming, which only heightened Jen's suspicions.

"What kind of issues?"

"I'm afraid I'm not at liberty to discuss that ma—I mean Jen."

"Then I'm afraid I'm not at liberty to grant you access to my property. You step foot off that driveway, and I'll shoot you myself, right after I set the dogs on you. And you," she pointed at Simone, "better make sure no one bothers me again until I see those boys on my porch." She spun on her heel and slammed the door. It was going to be a long day.

***

For more of Jen's story, check out Until You Came Along by Rose Bak. Available at select online retailers.

Other Books by Rose Bak

Boozy Book Club Series
Beach Reads
Bubbly & Billionaires
Martinis & Mysteries
Bourbon & Bikers
The Good with Numbers Holiday Romance Series
Love Unmasked
The Thanksgiving Scrooge
Maid for Christmas
Countdown to Love
Valentine's Lottery
Bite-Sized Shifters Paranormal Romance Series
Long Distance Wolf
Wolf Doctor
Kat's Dog
Designer Wolf
Wolf Sheriff
Cocktail Wolf
Second Chance Wolf
The Oliver Boys Band Contemporary Romance Series
Until You Came Along
Rock Star Teacher
Rock Star Writer
Rock Star Neighbor
Rock Star Lawyer
Loving the Holidays Contemporary Romance Series
Dating Santa
New Year's Steve
Independence Dave
Holidays with the Shifters Series

Santa's Claws
Bear Humbug
Jingle Bear
Silver Paws
Joy to the Wolf
Lion's Heart
The Diamond Bay Contemporary Romance Series
Brand New Penny
Fresh as a Daisy
Right as Rain
Reunited Series
Together Again
Finding My Baby
Beach Wedding
Non-fiction
What to Do If You Find a Cougar in Your Living Room: Self-Care in an Uncaring World
It's All About Relationships: Reflections on Love, Friendship, and Connection

Catch up with these and other stories coming soon. Join my newsletter for more information[1] or follow my author page on your favorite retailer.

---

1. *https://storyoriginapp.com/giveaways/62ee758e-068f-11eb-904e-c373f6014fe1*

About the Author

Rose Bak has been obsessed with books since she got her first library card at age five. She is a passionate reader with an e-reader bursting with thousands of beloved books.

Although Rose enjoys writing both fiction and nonfiction, romance novels have always been her favorite guilty pleasure, both as a reader and an author. Rose's contemporary romance books focus on strong female characters over thirty-five and the alpha males who love them. Expect a lot of steam, a little bit of snark, and a guaranteed happily ever after.

Rose lives in the Pacific Northwest with her family, and special needs dogs. In addition to writing, she also teaches accessible yoga and loves music. Sadly, she has absolutely no musical talent, so she mostly sings in the shower.

You can also follow Rose on Facebook[1], Instagram[2], Twitter[3], Goodreads[4], or Bookbub[5].

Please sign up for the Rose Bak Romance newsletter[6] to get a free book and keep up to date on all the latest news.

---

1. https://www.facebook.com/AuthorRoseBak

2. https://www.instagram.com/authorrosebak/

3. https://twitter.com/AuthorRoseBak

4. https://www.goodreads.com/authorrosebak

5. https://www.bookbub.com/authors/rose-bak

6. *https://storyoriginapp.com/giveaways/62ee758e-068f-11eb-904e-c373f6014fe1*

Don't miss out!

Visit the website below and you can sign up to receive emails whenever Rose Bak publishes a new book. There's no charge and no obligation.

https://books2read.com/r/B-A-VATM-KZIZB

BOOKS 2 READ

Connecting independent readers to independent writers.

Did you love *Martinis & Mysteries*? Then you should read *Beach Reads*[7] by Rose Bak!

She was supposed to be celebrating her sister's birthday, not falling in love with some guy she just met!

When her sister invites her on a girls' weekend to celebrate her fiftieth birthday, Teresa tries her best to get out of it. She's much too busy to take a vacation, let alone spend time with the charming and sexy bartender at the resort they're visiting.

Colin never believed in love at first sight, at least until he set eyes on Teresa. The curvy beauty is everything he's ever wanted in a woman. If he could just convince her to stay...but first, he needs to tell her the truth about who he really is.

It's not just a vacation fling...it's love.

---

7. https://books2read.com/u/3LVKOe

8. https://books2read.com/u/3LVKOe

"Beach Reads" is a prequel novella in the "Boozy Book Club" series. Each story in the series is a steamy standalone featuring a couple over forty-five, a nosy group of matchmaking friends, and a sweet happily ever after that proves anyone can find love later in life.

Read more at https://rosebakenterprises.com/.